Millions of Americans remember Dick and Jane (and Sally and Spot too!). The little stories with their simple vocabulary words and warmly rendered illustrations were a hallmark of American education in the 1950s and 1960s.

But the first Dick and Jane stories actually appeared much earlier—in the Scott Foresman Elson Basic Reader Pre-Primer, copyright 1930. These books featured short, upbeat, and highly readable stories for children. The pages were filled with colorful characters and large, easy-to-read Century Schoolbook typeface. There were fun adventures around every corner of Dick and Jane's world.

Generations of American children learned to read with Dick and Jane, and many still cherish the memory of reading the simple stories on their own. Today, Pearson Scott Foresman remains committed to helping all children learn to read—and love to read. As part of Pearson Education, the world's largest educational publisher, Pearson Scott Foresman is honored to reissue these classic Dick and Jane stories, with Grosset & Dunlap, a division of Penguin Young Readers Group. Reading has always been at the heart of everything we do, and we sincerely hope that reading is an important part of your life too.

Dick and Jane is a registered trademark of Addison-Wesley Educational Publishers, Inc.
From GUESS WHO. Copyright © 1951 by Scott Foresman and Company, copyright renewed
1979. From THE NEW WE WORK AND PLAY. Copyright © 1956 by Scott Foresman and
Company, copyright renewed 1984. All rights reserved. Published by Grosset & Dunlap,
a division of Penguin Young Readers Group, 345 Hudson Street, New York, NY, 10014.
GROSSET & DUNLAP is a trademark of Penguin Group (USA) Inc. Published simultaneously
in Canada. Printed in the U.S.A.

*Library of Congress Cataloging-in-Publication Data is available.*

ISBN 0-448-43404-0 (pbk)     B C D E F G H I J

ISBN 0-448-43416-4 (GB)     B C D E F G H I J

*Read with*
# Dick and Jane

# Go Away, Spot

GROSSET & DUNLAP • NEW YORK

# Table of Contents

# Jane and Puff

Oh, Jane.

I see something.

Look, Jane, look.

Look here.

Come, Puff.
Come here.
Jump, little Puff.
Jump, jump.

Look, Baby Sally.

Come here and look.

See Puff.

Puff can help.

Puff can help Jane.

See Puff Go

Come here, Dick.

Come and see Puff.

See Puff play.

See Puff jump.

Puff can jump and play.

Oh, Mother, Mother.
Come and look.
See Puff jump and play.

See little Puff play.

Look, Mother, look.

See Puff jump and play.

Oh, oh, oh.

See Puff jump down.

See Puff jump and go.

Jump down, funny Puff.

Jump down.

Jump down.

Go, go, go.

# Tim and Sally Help

Sally said, "Look, Mother.
I can help.
See Baby Sally help.
See little Tim help.
See little Tim go.
Oh, see little Tim go."

Sally said, "Look, Tim.
Look down here.
I see cookies.
I see cookies down here.
Cookies, cookies, cookies."

Sally said. "Come, Mother.
We can go.
Look here, Mother.
Cookies, cookies, cookies.
Come, Mother, come.
We can go."

# Go Away, Spot

Dick said, "Down, Spot.
I can not play.
Down, Spot, down.
Go away, little Spot.
Go away and play."

Sally said, "Oh, Spot.

We see you.

Tim and I see you.

And little Puff sees you.

We see you, funny Spot."

Dick said, "Oh, oh, oh.
Go away, Spot.
You can not help.
You can not play here."

Sally said, "Run away, Spot.
Run, run, run."

# Puff, Tim, and Spot

Sally said, "See Puff go.
Puff can jump down.
Puff can run away.
See little Tim.
Tim can not jump down.
Tim can not run away."

Dick said, "Come, Spot.
You and I can play.
Look here, Spot.
Cookies, cookies.
Jump, Spot, jump."

Dick said, "See Spot.
Oh, see Spot jump."

Jane said, "Mother, Mother.
We see something funny."

"Come here.
Come here.
Come and see Spot."

# Spot Helps Sally

Look, Spot, look.

Find Dick and Jane.

Go, Spot, go.

Help Sally find Dick.

Help Sally find Jane.

Go, Spot.

Go and find Dick.

Go and find Jane.

Run, Spot, run.

Run and find Dick.

Run and find Jane.

Oh, oh, oh.

Spot can find Dick.

Spot can find Jane.

Oh, oh.

Spot can help Sally.

Spot can play.